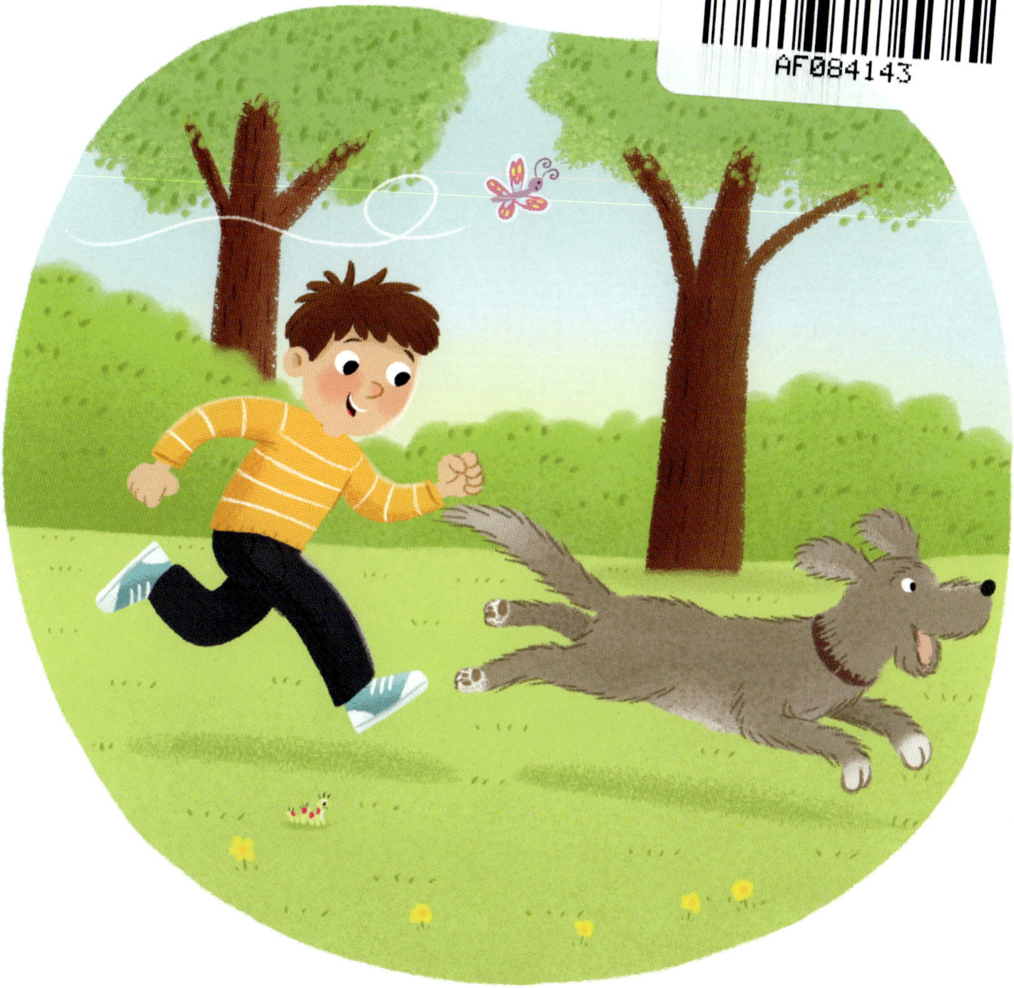

Zack and Rags

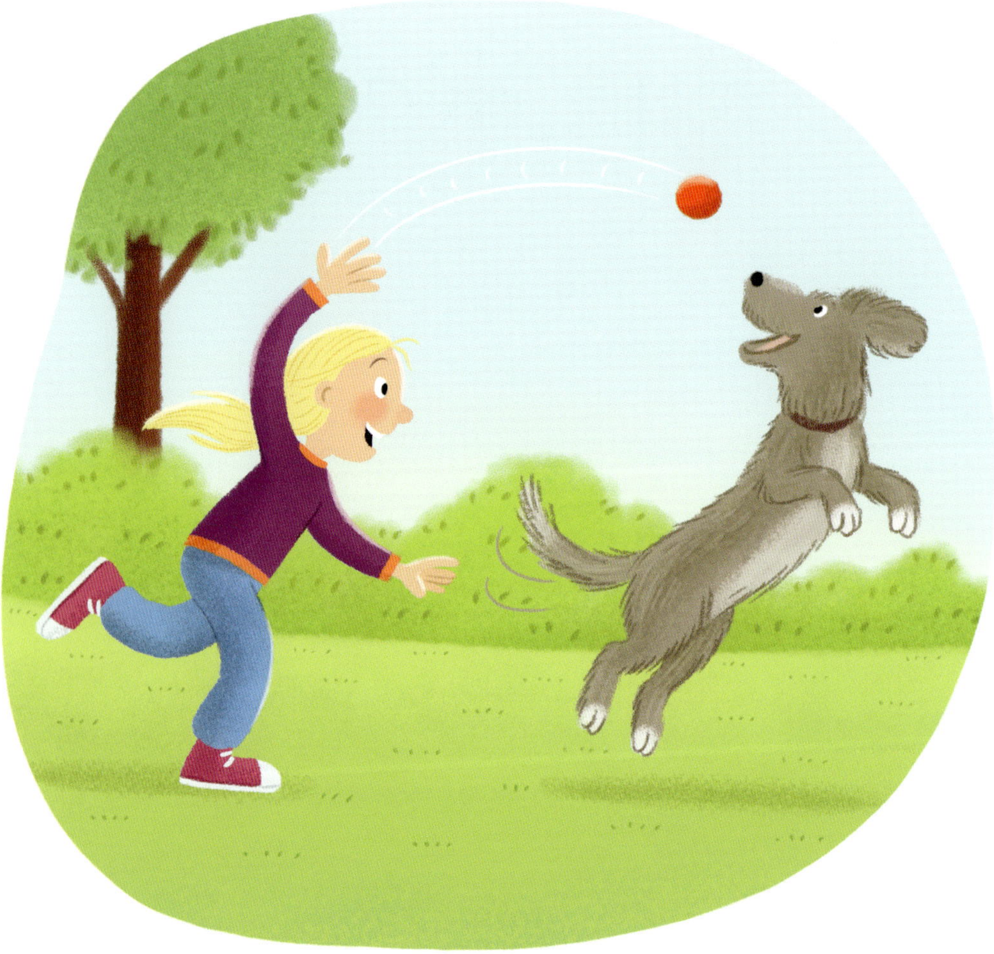

Jess

Run, Rags!

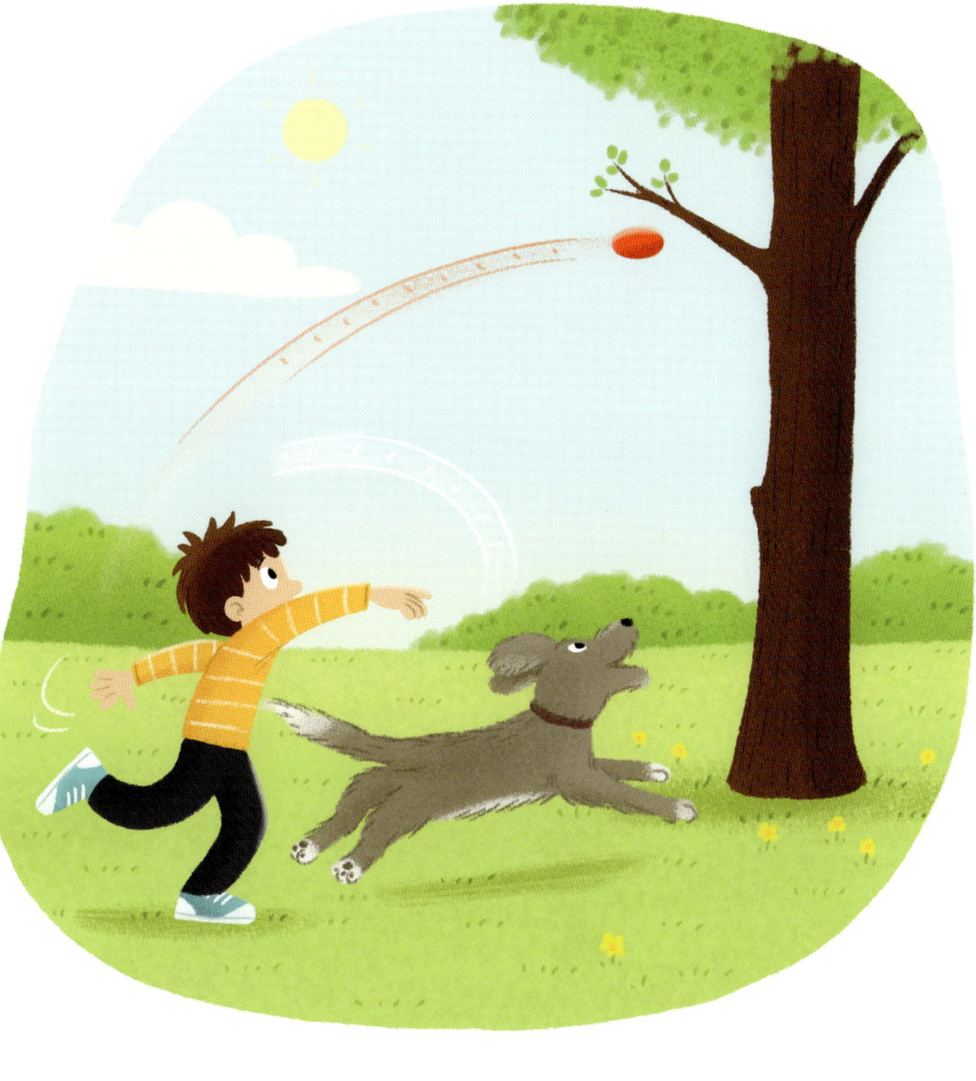

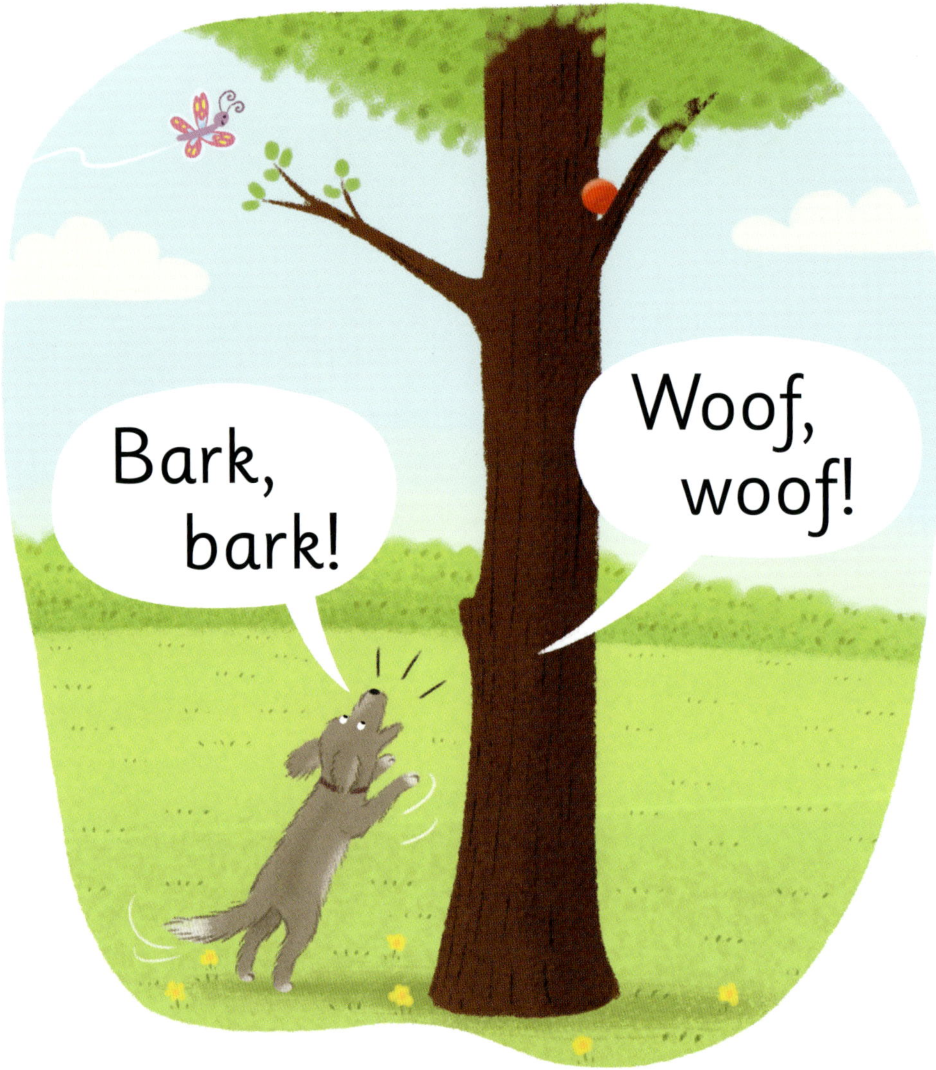

It is stuck.

"I will get it!"

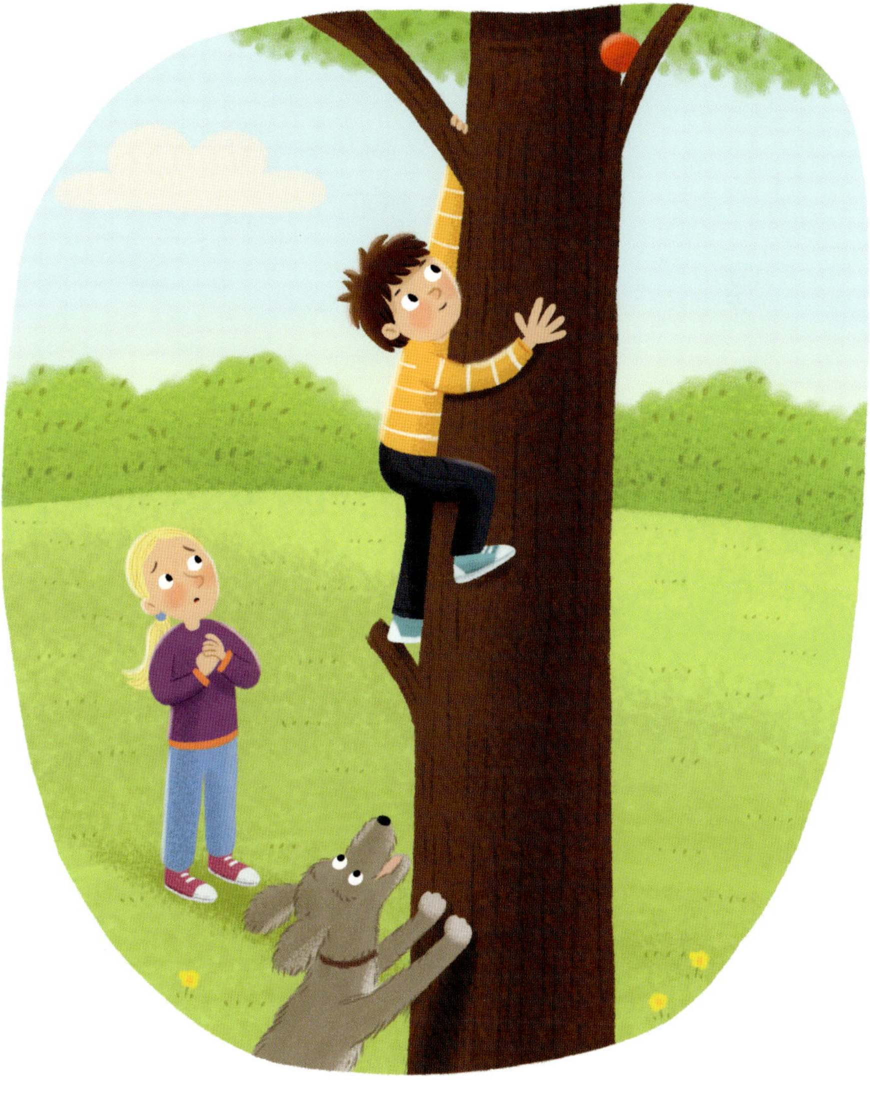

“Help me!”

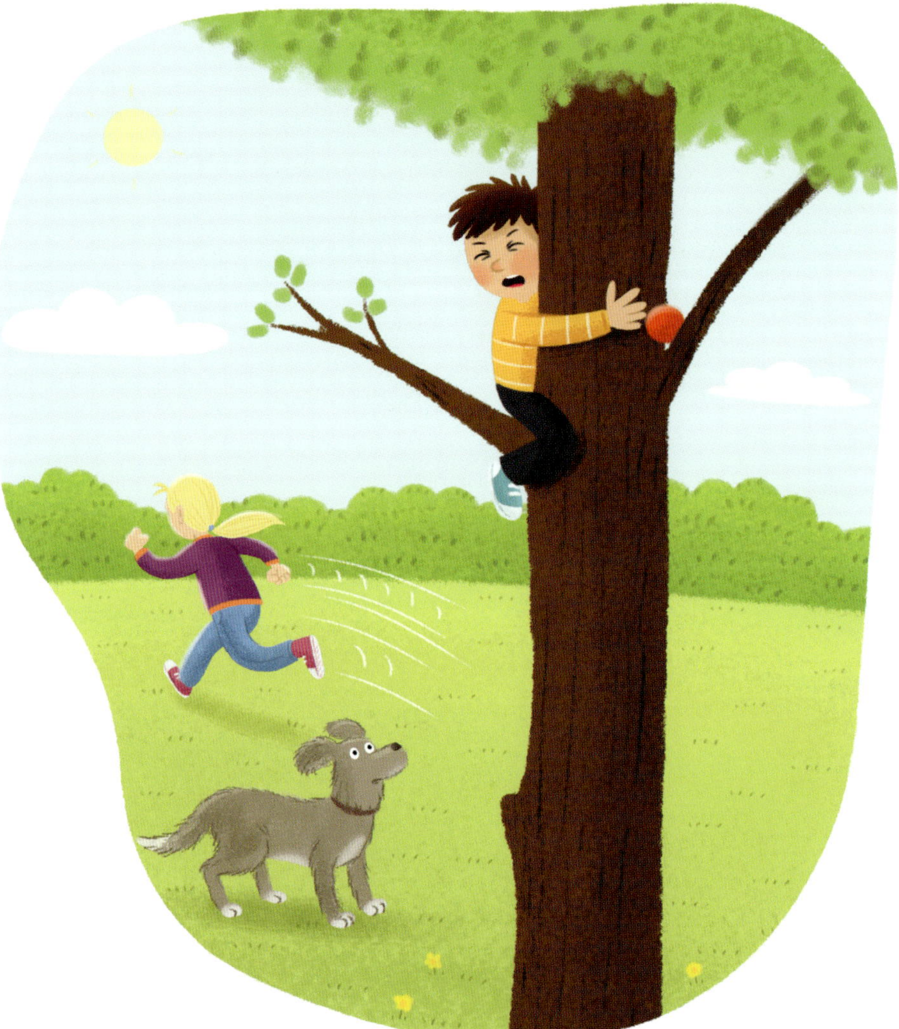

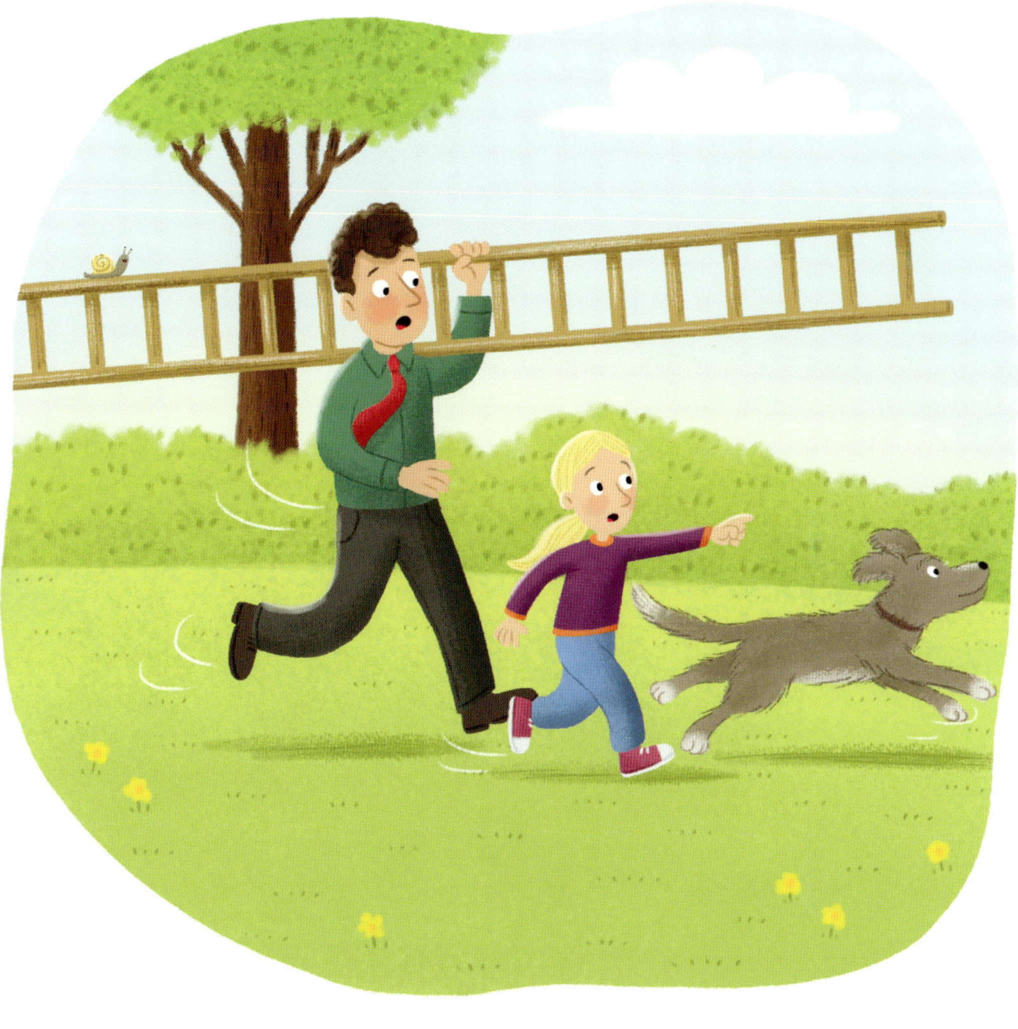

Dad has a ladder.

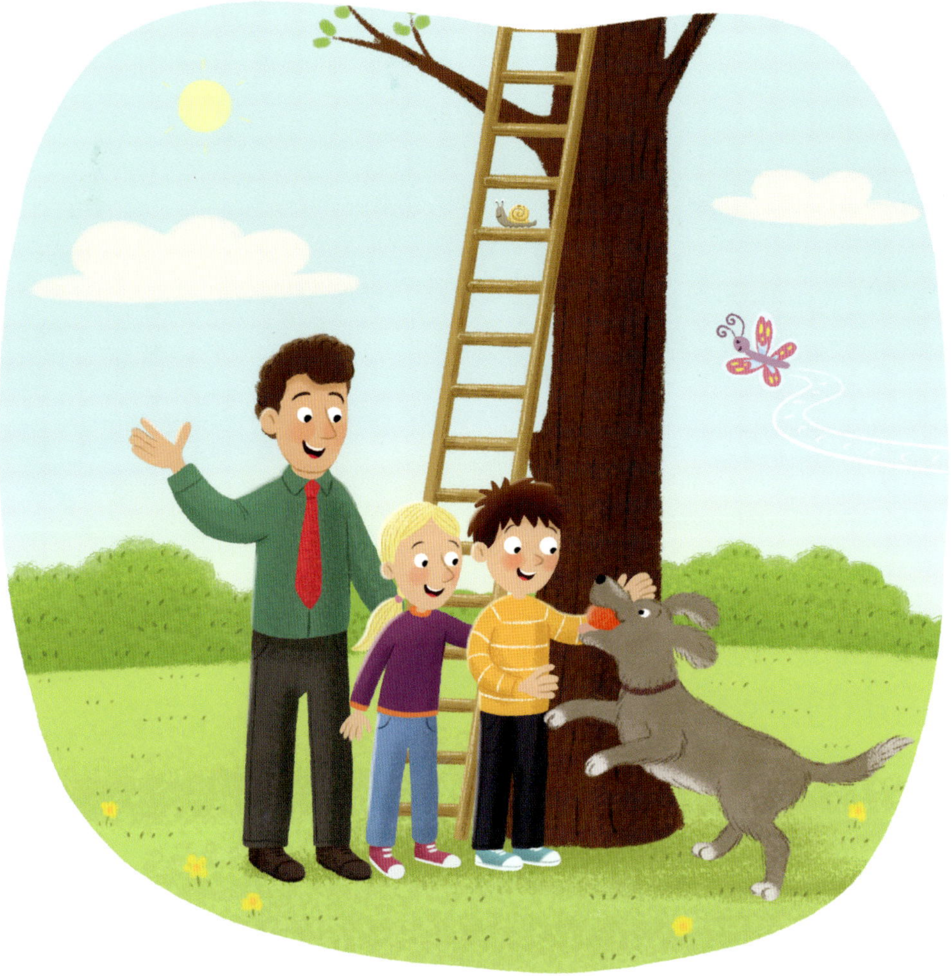

Thanks, Dad!